Welcome to ALADDIN QUIX!

If you are looking for fast, fun-to-read stories with colorful characters, lots of kid-friendly humor, easy-to-follow action, entertaining story lines, and lively illustrations, then **ALADDIN QUIX** is for you!

But wait, there's more!

If you're also looking for stories with tables of contents; word lists; about-the-book questions; 64, 80, or 96 pages; short chapters; short paragraphs; and large fonts, then **ALADDIN QUIX** is *definitely* for you!

ALADDIN QUIX: The next step between ready to reads and longer, more challenging chapter books, for readers five to eight years old.

Our Principal
Is a Frog!

Read more ALADDIN QUIX books!

Royal Sweets: A Royal Rescue
by Helen Perelman

A Miss Mallard Mystery: Dig to Disaster
by Robert Quackenbush

A Miss Mallard Mystery: Texas Trail to Calamity
by Robert Quackenbush

Our Principal Is a Frog!

Previously titled *The Frog Principal*

BY **Stephanie Calmenson**

ILLUSTRATED BY
Aaron Blecha

ALADDIN QUIX

New York   London   Toronto   Sydney   New Delhi

This book is a work of fiction. Any references to historical events, real people, or real places are used fictitiously. Other names, characters, places, and events are products of the author's imagination, and any resemblance to actual events or places or persons, living or dead, is entirely coincidental.

ALADDIN QUIX
Simon & Schuster Children's Publishing Division
1230 Avenue of the Americas, New York, New York 10020
First Aladdin QUIX paperback edition May 2018
Text copyright © 2001 by Stephanie Calmenson
Illustrations copyright © 2018 by Aaron Blecha
Previously published as *The Frog Principal* by Scholastic, Inc.
Also available in an Aladdin QUIX hardcover edition.
All rights reserved, including the right of reproduction in whole or in part in any form.
ALADDIN and the related marks and colophon
are trademarks of Simon & Schuster, Inc.
For information about special discounts for bulk
purchases, please contact Simon & Schuster Special Sales
at 1-866-506-1949 or business@simonandschuster.com.
The Simon & Schuster Speakers Bureau can bring authors to your live event. For
more information or to book an event contact the Simon & Schuster Speakers Bureau
at 1-866-248-3049 or visit our website at www.simonspeakers.com.
Cover designed by Karin Paprocki
Interior designed by Heather Palisi and Karin Paprocki
The illustrations for this book were rendered digitally.
The text of this book was set in Archer Medium.
Manufactured in the United States of America 0418 OFF
2 4 6 8 10 9 7 5 3 1
Library of Congress Control Number 2018930769
ISBN 978-1-4814-6667-7 (hc)
ISBN 978-1-4814-6665-3 (pbk)
ISBN 978-1-4814-6666-0 (eBook)

To my readers

—S. C.

Cast of Characters

Mr. Barnaby Bundy: Principal

Marty Q. Marvel: Bumbling magician

Ms. Marilyn Moore: Assistant principal

Keesha Johnson: Star athlete

Roger Patel: Top student and class leader

Nancy Wong: Hopes to be a zoologist

Hector Gonzalez: Loves making his friends laugh

Alice Wright: Kindergartener who always tells the truth

Max Berger: Excellent artist

Ms. Ellie Tilly: Kindergarten teacher

Mrs. Gwen Feeny: Third-grade teacher

Contents

1

Ribbit! Ribbit!

Mr. Bundy is the principal of PS 88. His students and teachers think he's the best principal in town.

One afternoon, Mr. Bundy stayed late at school to plan a

new assembly program. He was looking for a special visitor to invite when an ad popped up on his computer screen.

Marty Q. Marvel, Magician
My MARVEL-ous magic
will AMAZE you!

The kids would love a magic show! thought Mr. Bundy. He called **Marty Q. Marvel** and asked to see some of his tricks.

In no time, a man wearing a tall black hat and a magician's cape tripped into Mr. Bundy's office.

"**Whoops!** Marty Q. Marvel, here! Allow me to amaze, amuse and confuse you!" he said.

"Mr. Marvel, may I please see some educational tricks?" said Mr. Bundy. "I like my students to learn from our visitors."

"Sure! One math lesson coming right up!" said Marty Q. Marvel. "Watch my hat and tell me how many birds come out."

He began to recite,

"And a-one! And a-two!
And a-one, two, three!
Come out, birds!
Fly to me!"

Marty tapped his hat once. No birds. He tapped it twice. No birds. He tapped it three times. Not one single bird.

He turned his hat upside down and shook it hard. Not one single feather.

"What kind of math lesson was that?" asked Mr. Bundy.

"Um, I guess that was my lesson on zero. Let me try my science lesson. It's on **amphibians**," said Marty.

Before Mr. Bundy could tell the

magician he'd seen enough, Marty was waving his magic wand in Mr. Bundy's direction, saying,

"He lives in a wood,
In a pond, or a bog.
He used to be a principal,
But now he's a . . . FROG!"

Poof! Mr. Bundy suddenly felt small, strange and slimy.

"Ribbit! Ribbit!" he croaked.

He cleared his throat, then tried

Wh-What?

again. Thank goodness real words
came out.

"Wh-what have you done to
me!" Mr. Bundy **spluttered**.

"**Whoops!** It looks as though I turned you into a frog," said Marty Q. Marvel. "It's amazing. That trick never worked before."

"Kindly *un*work it!" said Mr. Bundy. He was hopping mad.

"Let me check my instruction book," said Marty.

He pulled a rabbit, some flowers, a deck of cards and a small book out of his pocket. He flipped through the book.

"*Buenos días. Muchas gracias. ¿Que pasa?* **Whoops!** This is my

Spanish dictionary. My instruction
book must be at home. I'll be right
back," said the magician, tripping
out the door.

2

A Talking Frog?

It was a long night for Mr. Bundy. The sun went down. The sun came up. There was no sign of Marty Q. Marvel.

Finally, Mr. Bundy heard footsteps outside his office. His

heart leaped in his little green chest.

"Good morning, Mr. Bundy!" called a voice.

Oh no!

It was **Ms. Moore**, the assistant principal.

I can't let her see me this way! thought Mr. Bundy.

He **scrawled** a note that said:

Family emergency!
Be back soon.

Then he hopped from his chair

to his desk, to the window and out across the schoolyard.

As Mr. Bundy watched his beloved students and teachers arriving, he considered his life as a frog.

Even though I'm small, green and slimy, I can still be a good principal, can't I?

He hopped over to a nearby pond to think.

His skin was dry, and the water looked awfully good. **SPLASH!** Mr. Bundy dived in for a swim.

Wow! *These frog legs are amazing!* he thought, kicking around the pond.

A fly
whizzed by.
Without thinking,
Mr. Bundy flicked out his tongue.

ZAP! He caught the fly.

Hmm, not bad, he thought.

At recess, a group of kids came

outside to play soccer. **Keesha**, a PS 88 star athlete, kicked the ball and it went flying!

Roger, **Nancy** and **Hector** ran after it.

"Uh-oh. I think the ball landed in the water," said Roger.

"What will we do now?" asked Nancy.

They heard a voice call, "I can help you!"

"Who said that?" asked Hector.

The kids thought the voice was coming from the water.

But the next instant, a frog jumped out from behind the **cattails** and said, "It was me!"

"Huh?" said Roger. "Frogs can't talk."

"You may think of me as an

exception to the rule," said
Mr. Bundy. "I am a frog. I can talk.
And I can get you your ball."

The kids could hardly believe
their eyes and ears. A frog wearing

clothes and talking? Things like this happened only in fairy tales.

"I would like a favor in return," continued the frog. "I want to be your principal."

"B-b-but we have a principal," said Hector.

"**That's right!** Our principal, Mr. B, is the best!" said Nancy.

Hearing that made Mr. Bundy proud. He wanted to continue being their principal—even as a frog.

"It's up to you," he said. "I will get the ball, but only if I can be your principal."

The friends stepped away from the frog to talk it over.

"He can't be our principal," said Roger. **"He's a frog!"**

"We can tell him he can be our principal, but we don't have to mean it," said Nancy.

"I guess it's the only way to get our ball back," said Hector.

So the three friends told the frog it would be okay.

"Do you promise?" asked Mr. Bundy.

"We promise," said Roger, Nancy and Hector, crossing their fingers behind them.

Mr. Bundy hopped into the pond and got the ball. He tossed it to the kids.

"Thanks, frog!" they called, running back to school.

"Wait for me!" cried Mr. Bundy. "I can't move that fast!"

But the kids were already too far away to hear him.

3

Zap! Zap! Zap!

That afternoon, Ms. Moore held a special assembly.

"Mr. Bundy has been called away. While he's gone, we must work together to—"

Knock, knock.

"Roger, please see who that is," said Ms. Moore.

Roger was pretty sure he knew who it was. He walked to the door and opened it a crack.

"Let me in!" croaked a voice.

Roger slammed the door and returned to his seat.

"Who was there, Roger?" asked Ms. Moore. "You look as though you've seen a ghost."

"It's not a ghost. **It's a frog!**" called out **Alice**, a kindergarten student. Like most of the kids at school, she had already heard about the talking frog, and Alice had a habit of telling the truth no matter what.

"Will someone please tell me what's going on?" asked Ms. Moore.

The kids told her the whole story.

"We promised the frog he could be our principal," said Hector.

Ms. Moore thought her students were joking. She couldn't wait to see what they were up to.

"A promise is a promise," she said. "If you promised the frog he could be your principal, you have to let him in."

Roger opened the door.

Mr. Bundy, the frog principal, hopped down the **aisle** and up to the stage.

Poor Ms. Moore almost fainted.

"**Ribbit** . . . er . . . good afternoon," croaked the frog. "I've heard that Mr. Bundy is an excellent principal. I will do my best to fill his shoes while he's gone. Of course, they may be a little large for me. **Ha, ha!**"

No one else laughed. They were too stunned.

"It must be a computer trick," whispered one of the teachers.

"It's probably a **hologram**," another teacher said.

"It will be business as usual until Mr. Bundy returns," continued the frog principal. "In fact, you may call me Mr. B."

After the assembly, Mr. B made his school rounds, hopping up and down the halls. He was almost **trampled** by two students racing by.

"No running in the halls, please!" called Mr. Bundy.

The students, Keesha and **Max**, stopped and looked around.

"Hey, kids, I'm down here!"

Mr. Bundy reminded them.

Max looked down. "This is so weird," he whispered to Keesha.

"No kidding," said Keesha. "We almost squished our principal!"

Mr. Bundy visited the gym first. Some students were playing leapfrog, and he couldn't resist.

He hopped in, leaped over Hector's shoulders, then hopped back out.

"Please tell me that didn't happen," said Hector, rolling his eyes.

"Of course it happened," said Roger. **"Our principal is a frog!"**

After gym, Mr. Bundy showed up at **Ms. Tilly**'s kindergarten class where they were learning about water.

"Hello, Mr. B!" called the students.

"Hi, everyone!" answered Mr. Bundy.

The next thing they knew— **SPLASH!**—their principal was swimming laps in the sink. They tried their best not to giggle.

"Very refreshing," said Mr. Bundy, hopping out.

"Here, Mr. B," said Alice. She handed him a paper towel to dry off.

"Thank you very much," said

Mr. Bundy. He went out the door, leaving a trail of small puddles behind him.

Next, Mr. Bundy visited **Mrs. Feeny**'s class. They were in the middle of a science lesson. Nancy held a shoebox with holes poked in the top.

"What have you got there?" asked Mr. Bundy.

Nancy opened the box to show him.

ZAP! ZAP! ZAP!

Mr. Bundy swallowed Nancy's bug collection.

URP!

"The principal ate my home-work!" cried Nancy.

"Mrs. Feeny, please give this student a gold star," said Mr. Bundy. "Her collection of bugs was delicious. . . . I mean excel-lent!"

4

Look Who's Back!

As the days went by, it was harder and harder for Mr. Bundy to be a frog. He couldn't go home because hopping all the way back and forth would take too long. He missed his hot shower and his cozy bed.

He also missed his own home cooking. Flies and worms were tasty, but catching them wasn't easy. They were so fast! **Buzz, buzz, buzz!**

Still, Mr. Bundy tried to be the best frog principal he could be. And the students and teachers tried their best to accept him.

Roger, Hector and Nancy were very sorry they had lied.

"We shouldn't have made a promise if we didn't mean it," said Hector.

"It's embarrassing having a frog for a principal," said Roger. "But I guess we deserve it."

"I want Mr. Bundy back!" cried Nancy.

Mr. Bundy heard his students and his heart sank. He had been calling Marty Q. Marvel every day, but there never was an answer. He hoped the magician would come back soon.

If not, I'll be a frog forever and ever, thought Mr. Bundy.

Then, one day at recess, Mr. B was watching a softball game from his office.

He was wondering how long he could go on being a frog principal when suddenly . . . a ball came flying through the window!

It landed with a thump on Mr. B's little green head. Stars were spinning in his eyes.

THUMP!

Out of nowhere, Mr. Bundy started reciting a magic spell.

"And a-one, and a-two,
and a-one, two, three.
Look who's back! Hooray!
It's . . . ME!"

POOF! Mr. Bundy was his old self again.

Ms. Moore heard the loud **commotion** and came running.

"Mr. Bundy! Welcome back!" she cried. "I was so worried

about you. Is everything all right?"

Mr. Bundy looked down. He saw his own two hands. He saw his own two legs.

"Everything's great!" he said.

"You won't believe who our substitute principal was," said Ms. Moore. "I'll let the children tell you all about him."

Mr. Bundy went to the window and waved. The students cheered wildly and were so excited to have their principal back that no one even noticed when . . .

Mr. Bundy swallowed a fly.

ZAP!

Word List

aisle (I'LL): A walkway between rows of seats

amphibians (am·FIB·ee·ans): Cold-blooded animals, like frogs, that have backbones and can live both in water and on land

cattails (CAT·tails): Tall plants with brown, velvety tube-shaped tops

commotion (cuh·MO·shun): Noise and confusion; a noisy disturbance

hologram (HA·lo·gram): A special kind of 3-D image

scrawled (SCRALLED): Wrote quickly and carelessly in a messy way

spluttered (SPLUT·terd): Spoken in quick and unclear splashes of sound

trampled (TRAM·pulled): Beaten down with footsteps or stomped on

Questions

1. Do you think it would be fun to have a frog for a principal? If so, why?
2. If you could be magically turned into an animal, which one would you like to be?
3. Do you think it's important to keep a promise?
4. How did the kids feel when they didn't keep the promise they made?

5. Marty Q. Marvel couldn't undo his magic trick. Have you ever tried to do something and failed? How did that feel?